First published by Allen & Unwin in 2020

Allen & Unwin
83 Alexander Street
Crows Nest NSW 2065
Australia
Phone: (61 2) 8425 0100
Email: info@allenandunwin.com
Web: www.allenandunwin.com

A catalogue record for this book is available from the National Library of Australia

ISBN 978 1 76052 529 3

For teaching resources, explore www.allenandunwin.com/resources/for-teachers

Illustration technique: Watercolour on paper
Cover and text design by Arielle Gamble
Set in Brandon Grotesque 32 pt
This book was printed in January 2020 by Hang Tai Printing Company Limited, China

13 5 7 9 10 8 6 4 2

MIX
Paper from responsible sources
FSC® C023121

www.tashibooks.com

ALPHABETICAL TASHI

Anna & Barbara Fienberg
Kim Gamble, Arielle & Greer Gamble

ALLEN & UNWIN

SYDNEY · MELBOURNE · AUCKLAND · LONDON

Welcome to the world of Tashi! No one has adventures like Tashi. And no one tells such exciting tales. He came from a land far away, carrying only his precious stories.

Now, Tashi's ready to travel back. Hold tight as you ride magic carpets and flying swans. Cuddle close as you meet desperate dragons, mixed-up monsters, toothy tigers and more . . .

With Tashi, you'll find it easy to learn your ABC. Turn the page and let him guide you through his wonderful world.

In a land far away,
you'll find...

A boy called Tashi,
brave and bold,

Baba Yaga the witch,
cunning and cold,

Chintu the giant,
    bigger than most,

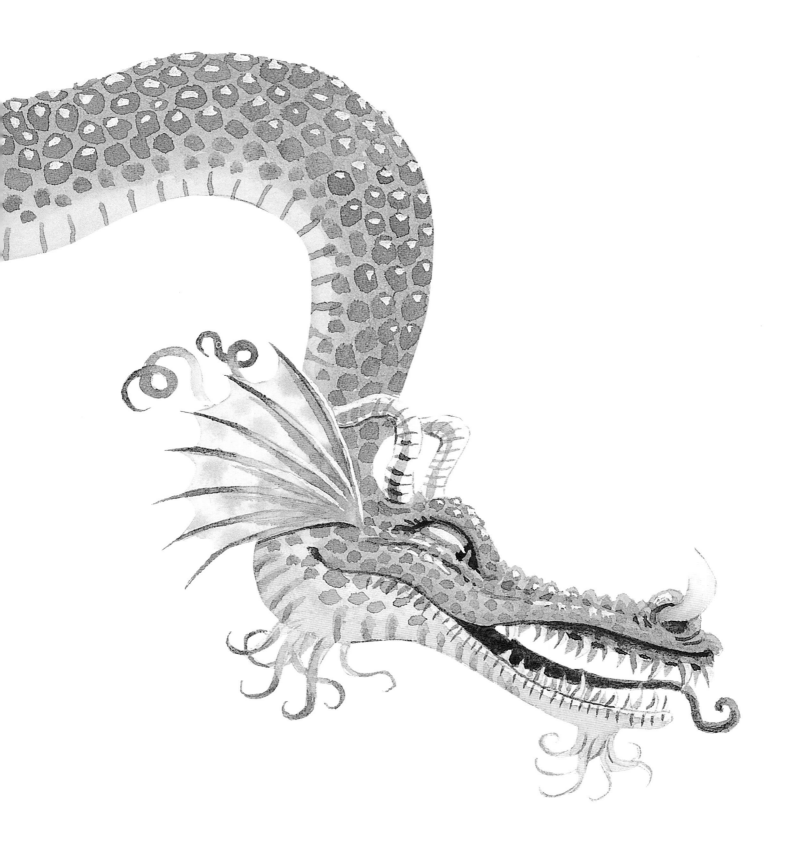

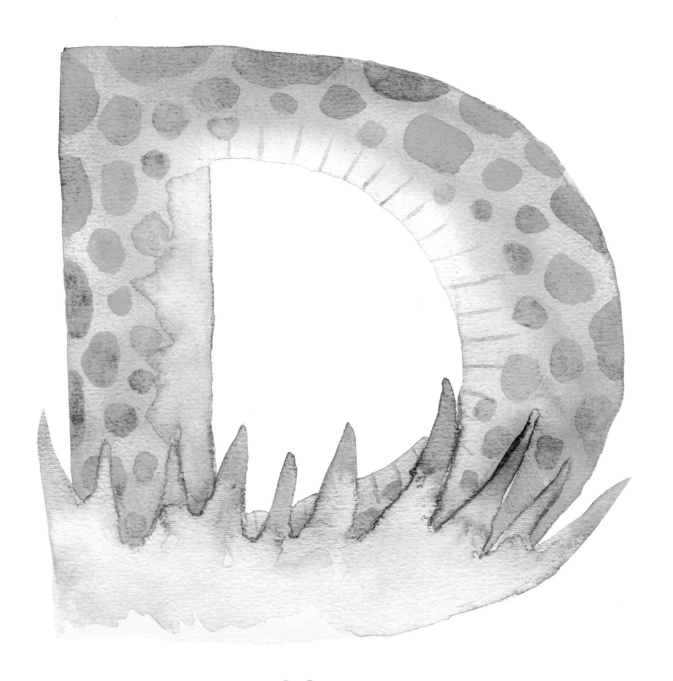

and Dragon of fire,
who'll turn you to toast!

In a land far away,
you'll see . . .

Eggs from dragons
of the precious past,

Flying carpets
    riding high and fast,

Genies who promise
to change your life,

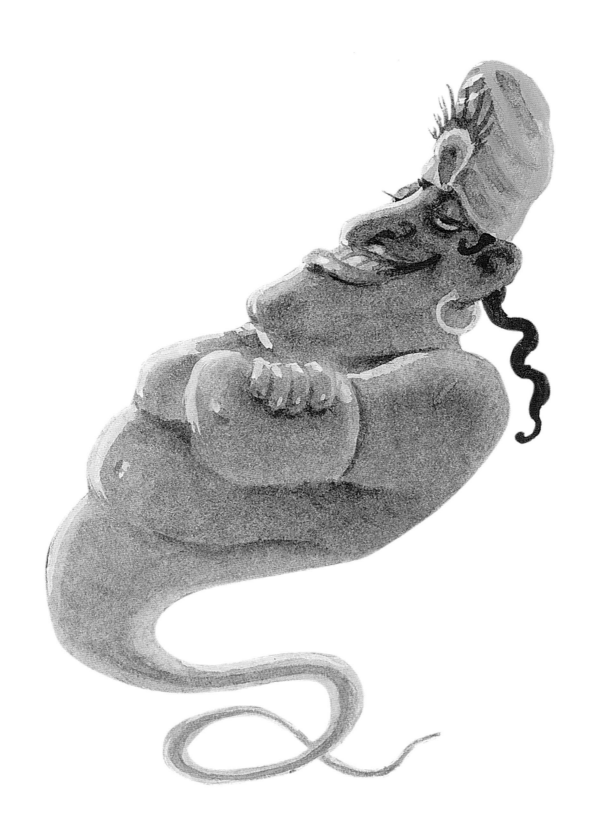

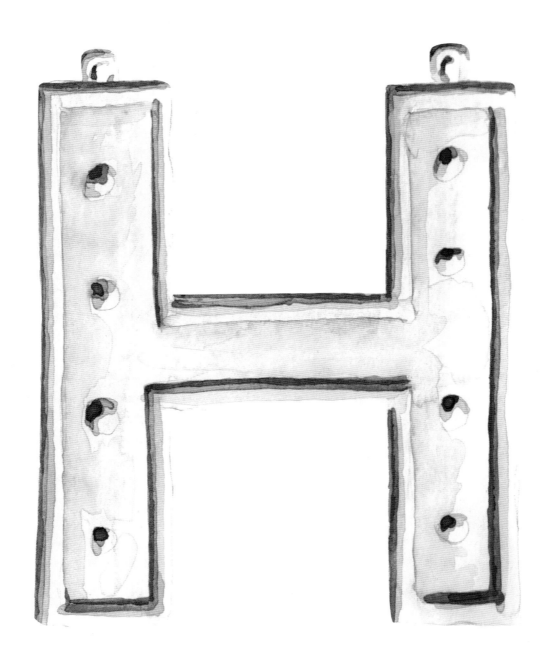

and Horseshoes with luck
to save you strife.

In a land far away,
you'll be...

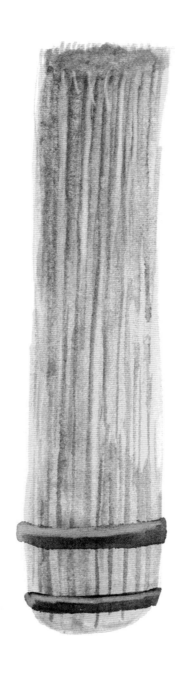

In danger of Soh Meen,
      that ferocious fool,

or Jester's rage that
bends to no rule,

Kidnapping Bandits
       on a hairy horse,

Lost in the city,
     scared of course.

In a land far away,
you'll meet . . .

Mixed-up Monster,
part goat, part lion,

Nervous Tashi,
    with an idea he's trying,

Ogre whose love
fills his eyes with tears,

and Phoenix who lives
five hundred years.

In a land far away,
you'll be . . .

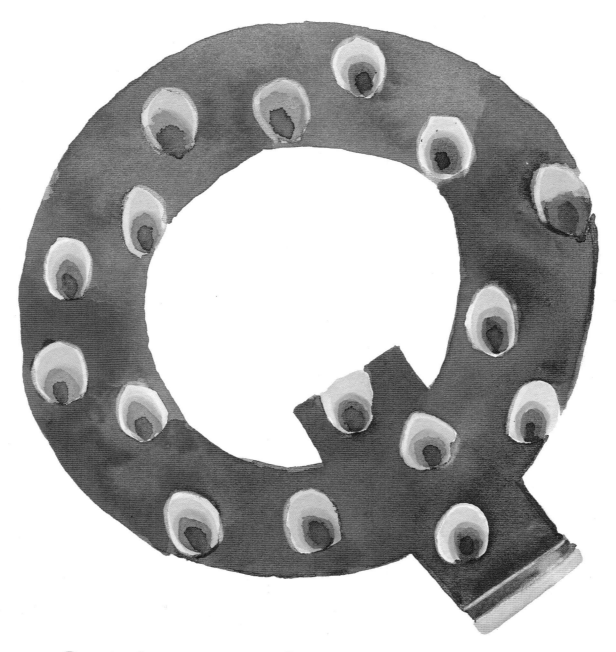

Quick to run from
demons that chase,

or River Pirates
coming face to face,

Swans escaping from
a war lord's fight,

and Tigers all striped
in black and white.

In a land far away, there's...

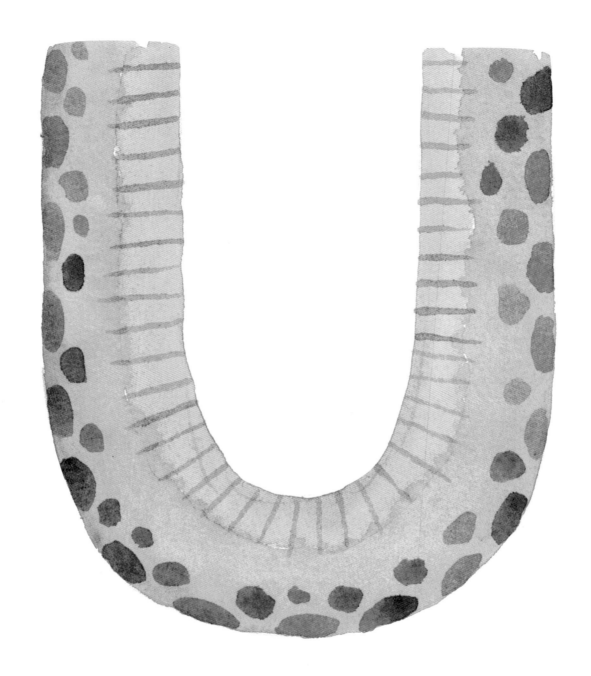

Upset Dragon, who's
desperate and doomed,

and Very Big Stinker,
　　who farted and fumed.

Watch out for War Lord,
Tashi's furious foe,

in Xi'an, where clay men
were buried long ago.

In a land far away...

Yellow bus roars
up and down,

and Zeng and his men
storm into town.

In this land of adventure and daring
Tashi is the hero, courageous but caring
and what could be better
than someone who's kind
whose heart is big along with his mind.

Tashi comes from two families, the Fienbergs and Gambles. My mother Barbara first saw him flying past on the back of a swan, so we brought him here to safety and gave him a best friend. And although Tashi told Jack the most marvellous tales, we didn't imagine Tashi would look very different from any other boy.

But when Kim Gamble got hold of him, Tashi turned from an ordinary boy who told magical tales into a magical boy. Kim shaped and dressed him, giving him a curious curl and a Santa Claus suit 'because Tashi carried magic gifts in his pockets'.

Tashi comes from a long line of storytellers. Since Barbara was very young, she told stories to entertain her friends (and get her out of trouble). And when she grew up to be a teacher librarian, she passed her passion for stories to me and hundreds of children as she read aloud to us in her library.

Kim too grew up loving stories, and drawing the heroes and baddies he found there. He also drew flowers when he couldn't contain his happiness. Kim and I met at *The School Magazine*. Our imaginations clicked and we went on to make scores of books. Like diving for a pearl, Kim reached in for the essence of a character, bringing it to the surface, extending feelings, transforming an idea into a world that was wilder and deeper than I'd ever realised.

I feel so lucky to have met this man, as do many thousands of children who've watched Kim draw a sunset, forests, moonlight over a river, all in the twenty minutes it took me to read the story.

And even though Kim is with us no longer, I am lucky that his exceptionally talented daughters have joined me now in Tashi's world. I've known and loved Arielle and Greer since they were little girls. From the time they were knee-high the girls' paintings hung amongst Kim's watercolours, blu-tacked up on his wall. As adults they've created their own paths across the artistic and literary landscape, and now they've brought their rich imaginations to join their father's, which has resulted in this truly family book.

We hope Tashi will become part of your family too.

Anna Fienberg

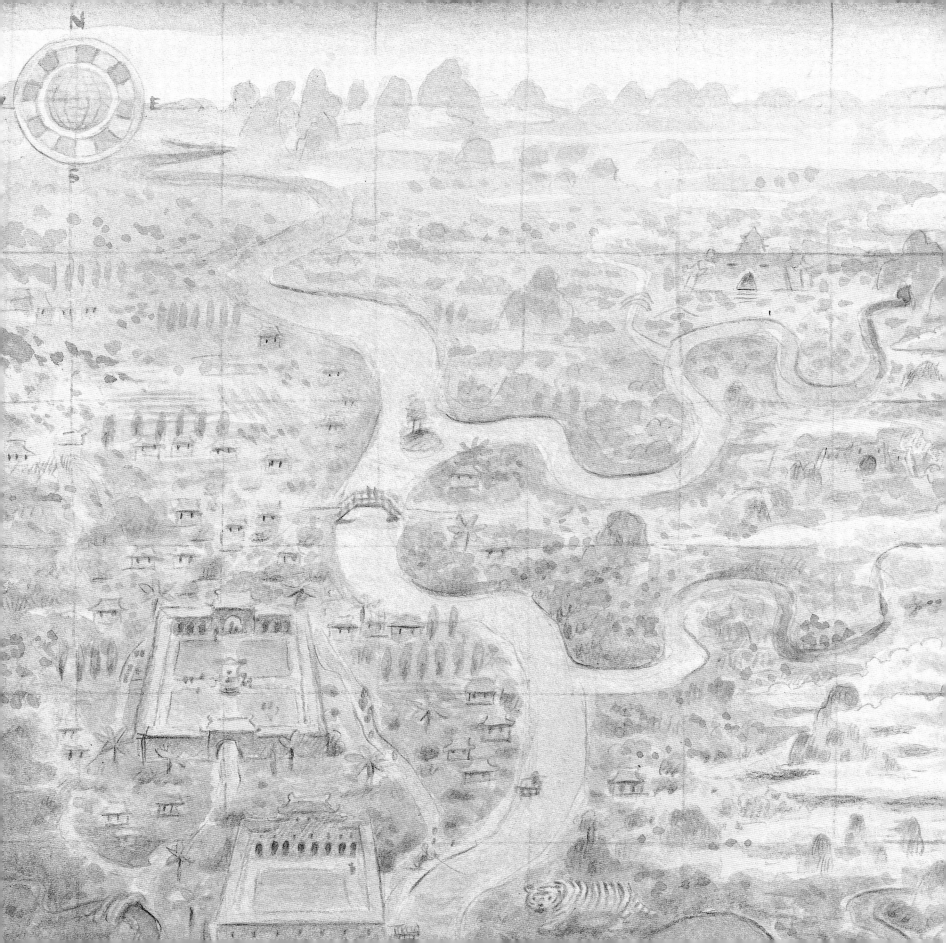